defiance

by Zsanece Brown

defiance

by Zsanece Brown

Copyright © 2022 Library of Congress

All rights reserved.

Cover design and photography by

Essentially Creative

Editing by Writ Publishing LLC

Baltimore, Maryland, United States

any of the above is an infringement of copyright law.

This is a work of fiction. Any similarity between the characters and situations within its pages and places or persons, living or dead, is unintentional and coincidental. The prose and author's notes include some names and identifying details that have been changed to protect the privacy of individuals.

ISBN 979-8-9874739-0-0

Also by Zsanece Brown

Poetry

Of Wishes and Dreams

by Kale Rogers and Zsanece Smith

(Limited direct sale copies available)

Sketch Story

A Shadow's Depth - audio

(Available wherever you download music)

For my sisters in spirit

Suzanna, Kim, Leva, and Genea

~ Table of Contents ~

Author's Notes

Prose

~ Preface ~

With undisguised irritation he told me that, instead of sharing the thought process behind my poetry, I should only say thank you in response to feedback. Letting people in was too personal, too intimate.

My writing though has always been cathartic. Early on, it became a door that I opened by way of an explanation and my readers are given an invitation to step through that door. I welcome conversation, shared insight, and unplanned discovery.

A finished piece was never meant to be a standalone statement. And expressing appreciation for reading is only the beginning. So, it's with a little bit of defiance that I choose to share the inspiration behind these pieces.

A Shadow's Depth

Sometimes

a darkened mirror

reflects with

unexpected clarity

A mirage

of deeper greys

forms substance

under scrutiny

~ S

1

Twelve hours from now will be the start of Twilight's Gathering. It's where Dreams go when dawn ascends, and the prospect of fading is too much to bear. Some though are inadvertently left behind and are never heard from again. Even remembrance of them is lost.

On the fringe of preparations, the forgotten ones are ever watchful. To stay behind by choice this time is more tempting than they dare say. Yet within them a dream's essence remains and the pull either way is great.

It has been Shadow's responsibility to keep these forgotten ones safe. And this she did from the moment they met.

She started out alone, so she thought. There were actually three Dreams who were separated from the others. The twins, Clarity and Mirage, stumbled upon Shadow along a cliff's edge. Stretched out on her belly, lying as still as a stone, Shadow watched the final stages of the gathering. The wind lifted her raven locks of hair in swirls and carried her silence across the valley. It was too late, and she was unaffected. The twins closed their eyes as the light brightened.

"The winds are picking up. We should find shelter," Shadow says.

She assumes the role meant for her and the others are comforted by this. Shadow finally turns and faces Clarity first. Clarity's angelic face has already been touched by the first shades of grey. Along her hairline and as marble it appears. Mirage takes her sister's hand and nods ready to go.

Along the path that brought them to the cliff are miniscule wishes, still shimmering and pearlescent. It is the dew their world drinks in. Normally the wind is but a breeze and it sings, softly and with warmth. There is a breathless warning in the words now.

"We must hurry," Shadow implores.

The trees along the edge of the forest part to show the way, the ruffling as frenzied as their footsteps. Wisps of Shadow's hair break free and rise as mist taking to the sky. Sensing her sister's longing to drift along after the dark mist, Mirage tightens her hold on Clarity.

"We're here," Shadow breathes.

She looks over her shoulder just as Clarity's eyes turn from blue to grey like a sky clouding over. Taking hold of one hand from each sister, Shadow turns her attention to Mirage and promises that everything will be okay as she steps backwards into the cave's open mouth.

2

Shadow can see them making the same mistakes as before. Dreams with troubled awakenings are accounted for but only in number. They are weighted and solemn. It has gone unnoticed, and Shadow is convinced that they will be forgotten too and that before long each will be a distant dream.

All of the Dreams drape themselves with indigo tulle, flowing and with frayed edges. The breeze whispers of Twilight and all eyes shine with unshed tears. Shadow allows hers to fall unchecked. Staying hidden away after the Dreams' return was hard enough but she didn't expect to see Aura, sun-kissed, as radiant as the others, and having forgotten all about her.

There is a pause in the breeze and its song falls below a whisper. The time has come for the Dreams to reflect on their awakenings, to remember where they came from individually. Their eyes drift close as the breeze returns, bringing with it a different song. For those who are weighted though, it's as if the breeze sings a mournful song and they are unaware that they've taken a collective step back. Shadow sees herself in these Dreams as uncertainty flits across their faces. Her awakening and theirs are not pleasant ones to reflect on.

Aura opens her eyes to a glimpse of Shadow stepping behind a painted depiction of Twilight's Gathering, vibrant colors on silk. The artwork hangs upon nothing and hovers a few inches above cobbled stone flooring. It is backlit by floating, twinkling wishes and stretches the length of the courtyard. In the painting, Twilight stands tall, his toned arms outstretched as wisps of ascending Dreams swirl around him. As Aura moves away from the group standing together, her attention is drawn from what she thought she saw to the details of Twilight's face.

His expression changes to reflect the Dream standing before the painting. His current expression is welcoming, and his dark, reflective skin captures the varied shades of blue of the Dreams' attire gathered in this open space. Aura is drawn to the almond-shaped eyes of Twilight and as she reaches out the silken fabric billows. The breeze is once again changing, signaling the eleventh hour. Twilight's expression mirrors hers and Aura smiles as she rejoins the others.

Shadow senses this shared serenity from behind the painting and wonders what to tell Clarity and Mirage when she returns to them. Shadow allows her hand to drift upwards to touch the silver trim that frames the image in front of her. The fabric pulls taut as if bracing itself. Twilight has not forgotten her.

As Shadow moves along the edges of the community, she sees that not much has changed since the last gathering. Dwellings nearly blend into the lush canopy of green, with elegant columns of pristine white carved stone peeking through to contrast with simplicity. Her home was where the iris grew only in striking and bold shades. And all of the neighbors wanted to know the secret.

She is drawn closer unexpectedly and finds her hand pressed to the door. With a sigh she slides her hand across and then down a cool plate of glass. Her home is opened to her again. The entryway has been redone and Shadow is facing a darkened mirror. She sees the same touches of grey streaking from the outer corners of her eyes that appeared along Clarity's hairline. And the strength that Shadow thought was hers seemed diluted. She wonders why this mirror has been placed here. Shadow steps back and, looking to her side, sees the family portrait still hanging. It was Twilight who begot her, but Aura gave Shadow her light.

It was this light that led the twins along the cliff's edge and to Shadow during the last gathering. Though she was found, Shadow felt that what she was looking for finally stood before her. Awakening from the depths of grey had left her disconnected from the Dreams around her. Shadow found her conflictions taking shape and, in Clarity, could see how much she truly wanted to drift away and disappear into dawn. Shadow spoke softly to Clarity while Mirage morphed into a soul mate. Time passes both quickly and slowly when counted as winks and breaths.

Mirage anxiously awaits Shadow's return, and his face relaxes as memories come to mind. His reality was different from other Dreams. His purpose, to bring about change and even embody this change. So as Clarity began to fade as the grey that touched her spread, Shadow lost some of her indifference and feared that she would soon follow. It was then that Mirage had to choose.

Shadow looked to Mirage as soft features slowly changed and a stiff breeze whisked away long, auburn waves leaving behind soft, short curls. Taking hold of Shadow's hand, Mirage completes a metamorphosis that forever links them. Some of Shadow's grey is now his.

Twilight watches Shadow's unease as she backs away. But as she turns from the portrait and sees Twilight observing, strength is drawn from her connection to Mirage and the darkness in her eyes begins to swirl. Though part of her is borne of a troubled awakening, she will not embrace only this.

Twilight's slight smile as he steps back into the portrait reflects Shadow's smile. Let the rest of them run from daybreak.

Poetry

distill'd

"But flowers distill'd, though they with winter meet,

Leese but their show; their substance still lives sweet."

~ William Shakespeare, "Sonnet 5"

My Love, while pent in dark and hollowed halls

away and far beyond our blended verse ~

where sullen glares demand a silenced quill

instead of beauty, scrawling speech so terse.

An essence lost is not an option, Love

Of yours nor mine, unspoken words assure

A comfort find and garner strength in troves,

for none removes our vested dreams of more.

Essential truths within our hearts incite,

inspiring whispers, casting doubt aside

A purer sweetness wafts and reaches you,

for tested love surpasses love untried

A silence lingers over pages shorn,

but none touches words of quintessence borne

fermata

you read like hesitance

and a pause that builds before collapsing into more silence

as my fingers trace your lines that steadily fade...

Thus, I rest on a page that won't turn

Your hold was like resistance,

staccato breaths pressed against my sighs

Though my hand hovered near your heart,

it won't yearn

And I swear I forgot to breathe

when I thought you'd touch me

Herein though there was promise –

desire tumbling into a swell. There's

assurance and there's hope within a pause.

In your silence, I hear

me – my measured breaths, slowed

exhalation and therein I swear I'm

lifted regardless.

untitled

Don't come down

Stay inside my eyes.

It takes too long

    to learn to trust again.

Don't know what to believe.

Don't know what to do.

Don't want to hurt

Anymore.

The rain is coming down.

My cheeks are getting wet.

Take your fist out of

My heart. Please

I can't breathe.

Don't want to hurt

Anymore.

untethered

tell me about your resting place

remind me of how you left this world

because of you I hated

that I wasn't strong enough,

that there was mercy in my floating above us

eyes fixed on the ceiling, not breathing,

briefly feeling the pain

I would give to no one else,

the pain I would keep to myself

I stepped away from myself,

but I learned that I could drift

when the world goes quiet

when my world goes dark

And I would wake moments later

hours later

years later

I used to think that I'd been broken,

that I'd been split in two

so that one could protect the other

until I got home

until I was safe

With a mask of pretense,

they mirror your feelings

Painted-on faces cover over

what is really underneath them

Only then can you objectively confront

what is inside of you

Perceiving it altogether different

from the next person, me

They can hide it all,

painting on a smile only if they want to

And so many others

would find themselves smiling too

Or they could create a look

of one disheartened

Only to make you feel

that you are not alone

Some show no emotion whatsoever

making it look so easy

Holding their heads erect,

they could take on the world

And leave all those

who would have liked to stop them

standing in awe

Whatever it may be they are trying to project

It leaves one feeling lighthearted

as the music slowly dies

Once the masks are removed and the

painted-on faces are washed away

The music and the many images stirred by

the painted-on faces never fade completely

Everything was all tucked

neatly away inside of you

They just helped you let it out

for a little while

The Dark Place

Some bad dreams are never forgotten

They just hide and wait for unsuspecting you

In the dark place

When confidence is at its highest

And all the badness is almost forgotten

You slip and fall

And end up looking face to face

With the dark place

Closing your eyes to delay the inevitable is

pointless

It all started in your mind

A few moments ago

Too late to erase now

The dark place looms before you

Forcing you to remember

Making you run... again

With all of the imaginary strength you can muster

Its shadowy fingers reach out to grab you

It has a face now

It has a name

The dark place is your fear, personified

The leaden box with the rusted lock

Heavy with bad dreams

Is hidden in the back of your mind

In the dark place

One defiant dream always manages to slip out

Wreaking havoc of the peace of mind

You've been trying so hard to maintain

Making you peek around dark corners

Be suspicious of those who call themselves friends

Be afraid

Always be afraid

The dark place makes you do this

There's no where to run to

There's no where to hide

Because the dark place is part of you

in the little corners of your mind

Get a bigger box with a new, stronger lock

Get ropes. Get chains. Anything.

Keeping the memories, the bad dreams,

The dark place away

Won't be easy

No way near easy

Revisiting Autumn

This is my song and I'm revisiting Autumn

to find joy in the place I once sighed,

to find peace in the place I once cried.

I hear the piano,

but I see a murmuring brook.

I feel cooler breezes in the shifting of seasons

and when a mournful cello joins,

there's warmth, auburn notes, and verses for
sienna.

This is my song and I'm revisiting Autumn

where you taught me to find comfort in nature

whenever darker blues crept into my dreams.

I was the cello.

I hear the piano.

I see your poetry.

And this convergence is amazing.

It's overwhelming.

So much so that I haven't listened in a while.

I get lost in the swell, those gradually
increasing sounds

Of Autumn. Healing. And peace, everlasting.

But for you, I'd play it again.

I would revisit this.

This is my song.

"Not all _____"

I listen to it all

The silences so tangible that I feel another's held breath

The responses so wrapped in rebuttal that they feel dull

Unresponsive in fact

Miss you with the expression of pain I guess

Did you listen at all?

Did you simply pause waiting for your chance to say, "Not all ____"

Holding my breath when I send my child to the store

My beautiful, brown child who towers over me

His quiet soul wrapped in a black hoodie

Hands in his pockets. Lump in my throat

Until he comes back to me

Miss you with the expression of fear I guess

Do you feel me at all?

Did your eyes just roll thinking to yourself, "Not all _____ "

Minding my own until I make it to where I'm headed

Dressed as I choose. Focused how I choose.

My quiet soul wrapped in thought...

and my experiences, no doubt

My facial expression and response to your preferences

are up for discussion. Again, I guess.

Miss you with the expression of frustration.

But listen to your spin on "Not all ____"

It's ironic

It's so ironic how we get it

until we don't

We hear clearly

until we hear where we fall

Then choose responses that remove self from
the scenario

Forgetting how far acknowledgement goes

Not realizing how much calm can follow:

"I'm sorry that you've felt that way"

Romanticizing the "beauty" and the "strength"
found in pain

Miss me with that. Seriously.

I listen to it all

I hear how her words are explained... to her

I hear her pause and the weight of it

And when she hears the space to interject,

I hear her fully

expressed

thought

cut

short

With an outline of where her and my
responsibility lies

Beautifully expressed, sis

Your pain is beautiful... I guess.

Mourning Autumn

there are rarely extremes
in the weather here
but that, I realize,
has resulted in the lack of brilliance

the heavy downpours are missed
by thirsty roots
and the early season chill
is sadly missing
...both sorely needed for my inspiration,
the breathtaking colors of Autumn

reduced to a breath exhaled
a mere few weeks it seems...
as Summer extends its hold
long after backpacks are filled
for the first time in months

suddenly and as an afterthought

a cooler breeze comes
with a burst of color

and as a burst expands
and then contracts,
a strong gust strips away
much of Autumn

just a week ago
a maple's red leaves fell
as in a pause,
but she was full...

today, darkened remnants lie
shriveled
and blood red,
carpeting and choking the lawn

scrawling limbs, bare
outstretched, gray and cold
almost beseeching
much too soon...

it was too soon

another strong wind sends
dried leaves scampering down the black street
eerily running
and
easily giving up

where can one go
if Winter is

just around the corner

Crashing Into You

When I first sensed you,

It was the softest blue I knew

~ Luminescent

and edged in

the purest turquoise.

But when I touched you,

I found it to be

the most peaceful crash

I would know

~ So silent

and edged in

searing white.

cadence

your fingertips graze my lips

tentatively... the moment a sigh

escapes me, shaken... aflutter

stirred as your gaze caresses,

traces the curve of this smile

softly growing... and knowing

intensity mounts with patience.

And words tempt me when whispered

as pearls falling from my neck,

captured and nestled by my breasts.

Your eyes hold so many questions,

one for each button I unfasten

slowly, baring to me the strength

I knew of long before now...

resting my hand on your heart

as anticipation courses, rises...

brings me to a pause. And I

reach for you as our lips touch,

your whispers blending with mine

just as I knew they would... as

surely as your firm assurance

is revealed, held here in my hand.

Guiding you to me, lightly brushing

the warmth of my promise

to envelop you in silken pleasures.

So... immerse, Love, and fill me completely.

Grasp my hips as I arch

to receive you, but... then slowly

withdraw, slip your fingers inside me.

Make me wait just a few moments

more. Trace my parted lips with

fingertips moist with desire.

Let me taste where you've been

as you take me, again... Rising

and falling in perfect rhythm,

capturing cries of pleasure with kisses,

stealing my breath... drawing mine into

your being. Inhaling my wishes.

Tumbling from the crest of a wave.

Shaken. Quivering... Finding release,

geyseric and filling. Falling into

each other's arms completely sated

for now...

He was an artist

He was an artist and, for a while,

I was a writer whose back and

shoulders were a canvas

where he'd write notes to me.

And in silence I'd read his touch

and I'd listen to his fingertips –

words that spoke to me as if

they were poetry, words that speak

to me as whispers of memory

Thank You

I noticed something about you

The way you allowed me to unfold, find my peace

whilst sharing this space with you

and how that realization slowly warmed me

The slight smile that I wore grew comfortably

And I told myself that if I closed my eyes I'd surely fall. So...

instead, I exhaled until I knew how I wanted to thank you

The words were trapped behind my lips

You know how quiet I can be

But without any frustration, I just allowed my hands to speak for me

To whisper my thank yous

Up the center of your thighs

Lingering at your waist

Pausing for the permission in your eyes

You

taste

like

those lines of poetry that are only shared
privately

You feel like the tension building, shaken and
trapped inside of me

And I'm amazed by how much release sounds
like

Thank you

Thank you

Author's notes

A Shadow's Depth ~ (approx. 2003, 2005, 2008...)

This piece was originally just a short journal entry, the opening poem. "Sometimes a darkened mirror reflects with unexpected clarity. A mirage of deeper greys forms substance under scrutiny." It was one of those thoughts that I had to jot down. I didn't quite understand what it meant but it felt important.

The rest was a visualization of a passing thought. What happens to dreams when we wake? What if there was this separate plane of existence where they lived until we needed them? And would passing from there to here be something they'd even choose?

Before this piece, I'd only written poetry. I worked on capturing what I saw. But I would step away from this piece for long stretches of time. Sometimes years would pass before I'd come back to it. I wouldn't be surprised if "A Shadow's Depth" continues to grow with me.

distill'd ~ (1/17/2009)

This sonnet was a required challenge entry for an online poetry group. The instructions were to write an original piece inspired by William Shakespeare. The inspiration could be a poem, a play, a character, or theme. I was inspired by William Shakespeare's "Sonnet 5," my thoughts about someone I'd loved from a distance, and how I felt about the break we'd taken from writing together.

I dwelled for a while on the verses that still resonate with me. "But flowers distill'd, though they with winter meet, Leese but their show; their substance still lives sweet." Those lines reminded me of an older piece I wrote. The title was "Still a Rose" and I realized that I had more to say on the subject. For me, the verses that I loved from Shakespeare's sonnet meant that one's essence is not changed by time and circumstance. I wanted to see how Shakespeare could help me explore that thought more fully.

Sometimes, I have a lingering response to a single word. My eye was drawn to the word distill'd, and my thoughts kept going back to it. When that happens, I'll have the definition in front of me and I'll dwell on its meaning.

One of the definitions gave details about the distillation process for perfume. That process brought to mind a fairly dark movie on the subject that I found captivating and atmospheric. Looking for visual inspiration, I searched for images using a keyword I can't remember right now but that search yielded one of the film's posters. It's a soft and intriguing picture in its own right. But it also happened to be one that I'd already loved and had saved to my favorites folder. I kept that image in front of me as I wrote.

I chose "distill'd" as my title, but I also chose to present my title in lowercase. There are times when the words that I'm drawn to and that most accurately capture my thoughts carry more meaning for me and power than I'm able or ready to fully express at the time. So, I'll begin with a visual whisper – lowercase letters. The same can be said of the title of this collection, defiance. But a whisper is a start, nonetheless.

fermata ~ (5/11/2015)

I'm often drawn to contrasts and, in this instance, I developed a habit of listening to light classical music to counter loud, chaotic days. The two basically cancel each other for me and I'm unaware of either sound as I'm focused on my work. But one song always made itself heard and I would stop everything I was doing every time it was played. The song was "Cristofori's Dream" by David Lanz.

I realized that I wasn't just listening. I also deeply felt the song's elongated pauses and I found myself holding my breath for the duration of each one. In general, my breathing changed, and I would feel embarrassingly emotional. I had to see what these pauses looked like, so I searched for the sheet music.

On paper the pause was notated by the musical symbol, fermata. According to Wikipedia, "a fermata is a symbol of musical notation indicating that the note should be prolonged beyond the normal duration its note value would indicate. Exactly how much longer it is held is up to the discretion of the performer or conductor, but twice as long is common." Instead of having a lingering response to a word, I was enthralled by the spaces created in response to this musical symbol.

I needed to write to explore how those moments affected me, but I didn't write about just music. When I started writing about how it feels within a prolonged pause, I realized that I drew a connection between how these musical pauses made me feel breathless and how I responded to someone. There was this – I want you, but not really – push and pull that drained me. I learned that I had to listen to myself, and I believed that letting go would allow me to breathe.

untitled ~ (approx. 1993)

    This is the first poem that I wrote. I was sixteen years old writing about just turning fourteen. I was thinking about this poem while working on this collection, but I didn't expect to find a written copy. I can still see the original in my mind's eye – overly-rounded manuscript letters written in blue ink on wide-ruled notebook paper. The page itself felt like an encompassing stillness.

    I also remember that when I wrote the version shared here, I edited out the word "knife" and used "fist" instead. I was afraid that "Take your knife out of | My heart. Please | I can't breathe" would be too revealing. I was creating distance from the truth behind my words.

    When I first started writing, it was a release, and it was for my eyes only. But this rewrite was part of my realization that I would eventually share. Unfortunately, I felt that editing was necessary. At fourteen years old I was very aware of victim blaming.   Where were you? What were you wearing? Did you fight back? Thirty years later, too many of us still ask those same questions.

untethered ~ (2/22/2021)

Drifting is how I describe when the emotional part of me moves away from the physical part of me. It happens when I'm feeling more than I can handle or more than I can contain (I realized the latter recently). The first time was after a public breakup. I was left standing at a bus stop crying and when I stepped away from myself, the emotional part of me felt disoriented as everything started to spin.

The second time I drifted was during my rape. When I knew what was imminent, the emotional part of me floated above us so that I wouldn't feel him. It kept its back turned so I wouldn't see what was happening. The two parts of me stayed separate until I was a few blocks away from home though I felt somewhat disconnected for days. Ultimately, the rest of that school year became, and still is, a void in my memory.

Painted-on Faces ~ (1994)

As a teenager I collected clowns and porcelain masks. I know some who have a genuine fear of clowns, but I was drawn to them. One of my friends asked why I had a collection of them. "Painted-on Faces" was the first poem I wrote in response to a question.

I wrote about what I thought of as the clowns' perspectives. If they were performing, what roles would they naturally fill? My favorite clown was the only one who had a tear, but she didn't emit sadness. And I understood that contrast. I believe that I saw myself in her face.

This was also the first piece that I shared with someone. My favorite uncle at the time seemed taken aback. I was always referred to as "too quiet" and I think that many felt that I didn't have much to say. I believe that this piece was an expression of me observing more than we all realized.

The Dark Place ~ (approx. 1995)

"The Dark Place" was the first piece I recorded as spoken word. At the time, my writing style didn't normally lend to what I thought of as spoken word's flow. But when I read this one aloud, I heard and felt its natural rhythm. I couldn't perform it with an audience though. Everyone in the studio had to leave before I'd press record.

The recorded piece included R&B in the background and when they listened after I was done, they started calling me Lil Poetic Justice. I definitely got a kick out of that, but I'm not sure what they heard beyond the piece's flow and the music.

This was also the first piece that touched on trauma responses that was shared with others. Maybe I realized that I couldn't allow myself to be seen while I read and felt "The Dark Place." For a while, this was the poem I would share

when I wanted to offer someone a glimpse of
me.

I used to dread Summer coming to an end because I knew that I would go dark in Autumn. That time of year is connected to trauma, gaps in my memory, and recovered repressed memories. I've learned that the body remembers what the mind cannot but, according to a workshop hosted by bts_healingthepain with guest Jodie Tedder, "healing does not require us to regain memories and we don't need to pinpoint the exact reason they don't exist. What we can do is relearn nervous system safety in the present moment."

I had someone who helped me feel safe again, a poet whose favorite topic to write about was love. Their second favorite topic to write about was nature. They introduced me to a piano and cello duet by Brian Crain and YuJeong Lee, "Song for Sienna." I can see

Autumn when I listen to this song. Nature poetry and "Song for Sienna" helped me see Autumn as beautiful again.

"Not all _____" ~ (12/12/2018)

I struggle with writer's block more now than I ever did. Inspiration can be fleeting, so reading and listening to other writers is a great way for me to reconnect to the art. Writing is but one medium of many through which we express our vastly different views. There have been times when I've forgotten that and saw creatives as open-minded by default.

When I react to lines of thought that lose the shine of rhyme and metered verses, writer's block isn't a problem. On this night, I heard more of the same and the reason I take frequent social media breaks. Sometimes, we see social issues only as far as it touches us. This piece was written in response to open mic, the resulting discussions, and conversations we still need to have.

When I need to write but can't find the words, I look to challenges and writing prompts. This time I decided to try a freewriting exercise. The challenge is to write without stopping for ten minutes. Do not lift the pen from the paper until the timer goes off, even if this means writing "I don't know what to write" over and over again. Write nonsense. Write anything. Just don't stop writing.

First, I went for a walk. It was the middle of the day, and it seemed like everyone was at work or in school. The neighborhood was empty and quiet, so I was hyperaware of whatever caught my eye and whatever I felt. As soon as I got back home, I set my timer and wrote until the timer went off. "Mourning Autumn" is unedited and pure stream of consciousness.

Crashing into You ~ (3/30/2019)

Dream journal entry ~ October 2018

Title: 12:21

We were on vacation. Traveling by plane. I was sitting beside you at takeoff. I didn't fasten my seatbelt until we were in the air. There wasn't much runway. Middle of downtown, but not ours. The pilot did a dead lift, instant climb after a short run.

Something didn't feel right. The plane immediately began losing altitude. You were then sitting in front of me. The plane began to turn while falling and I heard you whisper, "Jesus." Very little time passed before we soft-landed upside down. You reached backwards to adjust my seat to make it easier for me to get out. Then you adjusted yours.

I woke up. I looked at the clock. It was 12:21.

Cord cutting visualization ~ 4/24/2019

I was wearing a white eyelet summer dress. Your spirit was like blue crystal and the shades of blue swirled and pulsed, lightening as we went through the process. The facilitator, a presence that felt like Mother Earth, was sparkling pale gold instead of shades of green.

My connection to you was more about realizing how I felt and responded to others' emotions. You were the first I noticed in this way.

~ Speak. Listen. Give thanks. Cut the cord. ~

Consider Goethe's Theory of Colours discussion of blue, my favorite color. "As yellow is always accompanied by light, so it may be said that blue still brings a principle of darkness with it. This color has a peculiar effect on the eye. As a hue it is powerful – but it is on the negative side and in its highest purity is, as it were, a stimulating negation. Its appearance, then, is a kind of contradiction between excitement and repose."

~ Of course, your spirit was blue. ~

cadence ~ (3/27/2008)

There are times when I don't just feel what I need to write. I'll see what I need to write and sometimes it presents as color. Once I was locked into the emotion for this piece, I saw pearlescent white. I watched the hint of reflected colors sharpen and form individual beads before falling in slow motion and in silence.

I also see the words sometimes. It may be one word or two words, always in script writing. When I locked into the emotion for this piece and before I started writing, I saw a single word – cadence. It was in lowercase, a visual whisper.

When the word came to mind without warning, I felt its soft rhythm and its intent to build was evident. The written expression of "cadence" was meant to take your breath away especially once your mind locked on whomever you desire.

He was an artist ~ (12/24/2019)

He had this unassuming way of being protective even when we were kids. The only person who ever walked me home from school influenced my understanding of what it meant to feel safe. We reconnected years later and very briefly. But he described one of our memorable moments as a canvas. And he said that we were the art.

Thank You ~ (02/17/2021)

The Epiphany Radio family welcomed me at
the beginning of 2021 after I finally stopped
hanging out on the sidelines. "Thank You" was
written in response to one of the writing
prompts for Wednesday night's show "The
Love Zone," hosted by La Perla Negra and Ms.
VIP. The CEO of Epiphany Radio, Author Larry
D Maddox – Forrealthepoet Douglass, created
an amazing track for "Thank You" and it
premiered the following week on all their
broadcasting outlets. I'm forever grateful,
humbled, and inspired.

Prose

Embracing Shadow: The Birth of Silent Dream
~ (9/30/2008)

The fading light promises another dreamless night. There are whispers within the shadows and I'm certain that I'm actually grateful for silenced image and thought. More than my share accosts me at dawn and, thankfully, take their leave at dusk.

Dawn

I often say that I miss who I used to be, and that whisper passes over my shoulder like a breeze. And again, directly overhead I hear regret. The hallway that I pass through is stark white and much too quiet, the only time that silence has unnerved me. I imagine finding myself cornered by him surrounded by all of this white. I smell lemons and it makes my stomach turn. It was the scent of the spray starch on his shirt, smothering me as I lost my voice.

I sense his presence now and the air feels stagnant.

I pick up the pace but, as dreams like to do, my movement is sluggish as if I'm running while submerged in water. The struggle is draining. My breathing slows and I feel like I'm drifting off to sleep though I'm fully awake and walking.

"I will always be your doubt... the one who stands between who you are and who you could've been."

I find myself sitting among friends, unsure of when or how I got there. I put a smile on my face because their voices are soothing.

Images

Raine asks what makes me so sure that who I am now is less valuable in any way.

I wasn't even able to feel hate or nod in

reparation when I heard that three bullets ripped through his body. All I could imagine was his little brother's face while huddled under him, protected by him. He must have been so afraid, and I worried about the scars that would be left from being exposed to that kind of violence so early in life. I couldn't focus beyond that thought and I had no answer for my friend's question. But sometimes having the right question asked of you gives you a moment of clarity.

I'm drawn to pictures of profiles and faces with downcast eyes. There's a feeling of softness and introspection. They also, for me, represent vulnerability left in the wake of darkness. I embrace these images.

Raine asks, "Will you embrace yourself?"

Dusk

The fading light promises another dreamless

night. But as promises like to do, and that's another story, the void breaks. Image and thought move freely but they seem to have lost their voices. Muted and muddied shades of undefined colors give life to questions, doubts, and even hope. Dreams come occasionally now, always in silence. And that's enough for now.

soul place ~ (4/13/2019)

I refuse... I refuse to believe that emptiness is normal, that less or loss is a given, and not quite is a way of living. This unnatural way of being disrupts my soul. This isn't home.

I struggle to recall how tangible breathing is meant to be, how time is a beautiful thing when writing on another's skin with just your fingers. Tips brushed in gold. Lips touched by gold. Awash in sunset's glow. Of one light. This home I know.

Coming Soon

distill'd (audio)

be•Cause

That Dude and His MOs

(excerpt)

That Dude and His MOs

by Zsanece Brown

~ . ~

Hey, 4am. It's me again. Ry and I have
been up for about an hour now. He's pacing,
but my mom calls it dancing. And I'm pretty
sure she's onto something because, with the
pacing, there's also humming and giggles. He
discovered Tchaikovsky at about 4 years old.
And I think that this morning he's experiencing
one of his jams.

Sometimes, I have a good 30 minutes of
indescribable silence before this - his joy. It's
when I stir a little and reach for my phone to
check the time. It's usually 3:33am and I'll
think, "Of course it is." Silence isn't heavy at this
time. Not at all. Instead, it's a slowly exhaled
breath.

When you have a newborn, you're told to
sleep when they sleep. But what if yours rarely
slept, seemingly refreshed after quietly relaxing
instead of napping? Maybe they also wake

with giggles throughout the night. What if those newborn months then stretched for 17 years? That's when 3:33am presents meaningful pauses.

Thank you for "listening,"

for receiving my thought process,

and for joining me in my defiance.

About the Author

Zsanece Brown was born in Baltimore, Maryland, United States in 1976. Much of her poetry is inspired by dreams and love, longing, and the comfort found in silence. Her work has often been described as bordering on the metaphysical, finding connections between seemingly dissimilar things.

writerscafe.org/SilentDream

Instagram: essentially_zsanece

YouTube: Essentially Zsanece